Go Away, Shelley Boo!

by Phoebe Stone

Little, Brown and Company

BOSTON   NEW YORK   LONDON

Last week a new family moved in next door. They unloaded a huge moving van in the night. It was *very* dark out, and I couldn't really see anything through the trees. There was quite a lot of noise, banging and crashing and thumping, and I thought I could see all kinds of strange things over there. Elephants carrying couches? Lions driving trucks?

"Get back in bed," my mother called up the stairs, "and don't start making up wild stories, Emily Louise. The neighbors are just moving in. You can meet the new little girl in the morning."

New little girl? I thought. Hmmm, was that the new little girl I saw climbing out of that moving van? *That's* nobody I'd want to be friends with. *That* little girl looks like a Shelley Boo. Go away, Shelley Boo!

"Go to sleep," my mother called, knowing I was up, peeking through the curtains. That terrible Shelley Boo probably eats nothing but peanut butter and Rollerblades inside the house and doesn't do her homework and makes up lies about being able to speak French and doesn't like to have tea parties or do anything normal and nice because her name is probably Shelley Boo.

At school she probably dances on the desks while the teacher runs around saying, "Take your seat, Shelley Boo! Take your seat, Shelley Boo!"

$2+2=5$

Boo!

At music time when we sing "Farmer in the Dell," Shelley Boo probably won't play unless she gets to be the cheese.

At recess Shelley Boo is probably the first one on the playground, and I bet she's a *swing-swiper*, too. Those are kids that like to pretend they're in a circus on a trapeze, and they push their swing sideways instead of back and forth, knocking into everybody else's swing, trying to do dangerous tricks. Hmmm, I thought, if Shelley Boo is a *swing-swiper*, I guess I'll have to move away.

On the way home from school, Shelley Boo probably rides in the back of the school bus and hangs her head out of the window and it's very dangerous. Then the bus driver has to stop the bus and shout, "Quiet down, back there. Don't stick your head out the window."

Shelley Boo probably sits back there, giggling with those giraffes and those rude zebras she knows, the same ones that try to bite your ears when you take your hat off on the bus and they are always trying to steal one of your mittens. Then when I come home from school and my mother says, "Where is your other mitten?" I'll have to say, "A zebra stole it." And then my mother will say, the way she always does, "Hmmm, that doesn't sound very likely. Are you making up wild stories again, Emily Louise?"

My best friend, Henry, will probably go over to Shelley Boo's house after school instead of my house because it will turn out that Shelley Boo has drillions and drillions of baseball cards. She'll even have a Babe Ruth rookie card. I think Henry would stand on his head for that one, and Henry is *very* afraid to stand on his head at all since his older brother told him if he ever did, all his brains would go to his feet.

"Go to sleep, Emily Louise," my mother called again. I would have been asleep except I was thinking how nice it used to be before that terrible Shelley Boo moved in. Mrs. Thatcher lived there in that house, and she was an awfully nice lady who always bought dozens of the doughnuts that Henry and I sold so that our class could take a trip to the Creatures of the Sea Museum. She used to say, "Oh, I'll take five dozen," and then Henry and I were the ones who got the glow-in-the-dark stars for selling the most doughnuts, all because Mrs. Thatcher bought so many. I think I'll write Mrs. Thatcher a letter and ask her to move back.

I wonder what will happen on Halloween. Mrs. Thatcher used to give out Snickers bars — big ones, not itty-bitty ones. She always invited everyone in, and she always said, "Oh, what a lovely costume!" when I was a beautiful fairy princess with pink wings. And when Henry was a drooling monster, Mrs. Thatcher acted really scared, and once she even stood up on a chair and pretended to scream.

Now on Halloween Shelley
Boo will probably be a scary
ghost. She'll probably go
upstairs and cut holes in her
mother's best sheet, two big
holes for eyes. She'll probably
cut them too big so you'll be
able to see Shelley Boo in there.
I won't be fooled at all. I'll see
those two big holes and I'll
know that it's Shelley Boo!
Henry will probably think
Shelley Boo's costume is *very*
creative, and then she'll give
him all the apples she gets on
Halloween because nobody
ever wants the apples (except
for Henry).

Then Henry will be all happy with his big bag of apples, so he'll go off trick-or-treating with Shelley Boo, leaving me standing alone with my candy in the rain.

The next day Shelley Boo's mother will probably say, "Shelley Boo, where is my best sheet?" And Shelley Boo will point to me, and then I'll definitely have to move away.

Sometime in the night I guess I fell asleep, though I can't see how I did with all that stomping and thundering and crashing going on over there.

In the morning during breakfast, we received a phone call. I was eating my Cheerios, pretending they were little islands in a sea of milk and my spoon was a boat. My mother was cutting coupons, and when she answered the phone, her scissors were going *snip, snip, snip, snip*.

When she hung up the phone, my mother said cheerfully, "You've been invited next door to meet the new little girl and have a teddy bear tea."

"What?" I said, holding tight to two of my best bears. But I had to go. My mother said it would be *totally* rude if I didn't.

So I climbed the stairs next door, dark and mysterious with newspapers blowing in the air and cats leaping out of the big empty moving boxes scattered around here and there.

When I knocked on the door, it sounded loud and scary.

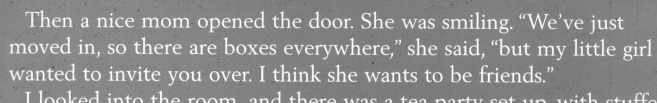

Then a nice mom opened the door. She was smiling. "We've just moved in, so there are boxes everywhere," she said, "but my little girl wanted to invite you over. I think she wants to be friends."

I looked into the room, and there was a tea party set up, with stuffed bears and stuffed elephants having tea, and there was a very nice little girl at the table, smiling at me. She said, "Hello!"

"This is my little girl," said the mom. "Her name is . . .

ELIZABETH!"

*For my wonderful son, Ethan, who, when he was little, taught me
all about baseball cards and glow-in-the-dark stars!*

Copyright © 1999 by Phoebe Stone

First Edition

Library of Congress Cataloging-in-Publication Data
Stone, Phoebe.
Go away, Shelley Boo! / written and illustrated by Phoebe
Stone. — 1st ed.
p.   cm.
Summary: Emily Louise, who enjoys making up wild stories,
watches the new girl move in next door and imagines all kinds of
terrible behavior for her.
ISBN 0-316-81677-9
[1. Imagination — Fiction.   2. Neighborliness — Fiction.]
I. Title.
PZ7.S879Go   1999
[E]—dc21   98-15788

10 9 8 7 6 5 4 3 2 1

SC

Printed in Hong Kong

The text was set in Berling Roman, and the display type is Benguiat.